Other Albert Whitman books
by Laura Bannon

The Gift of Hawaii
The Famous Baby-Sitter
Katy Comes Next
The Tide Won't Wait
Nemo Meets the Emperor
The Little Sister Doll
When the Moon Is New

WHO WALKS
THE ATTIC?

WHO WALKS
THE ATTIC?

Laura Bannon

AUTHOR-ILLUSTRATOR

ALBERT WHITMAN & COMPANY
CHICAGO

 LIBRARY EDITION

Traveling along the bay shore from Traverse City, Michigan, one comes to a sign marked *Bunker Hill*. There, in a house overlooking Grand Traverse Bay, the author spent her childhood, attending school in the small town of Acme.

This story, *Who Walks the Attic?*, is located in this region.

CONTENTS

CHAPTER 1

The Plopping Sound

HOLLIS woke in the dark and raised himself on one elbow. At first he thought he was home in Detroit. Then he remembered he was in a strange house out in the country. Mom and Dad had gone back to Detroit last night, leaving him and his grown-up sister to keep house.

Hollis felt sure he had been wakened by a thumping sound. He sat up and listened to the stillness of the old house.

There! That was it. *Plop—plop—plop— plop.* The sound came from the ceiling over his head. It sounded like some big creature plodding across the floor.

"Hey, Mike! Wake up!" Hollis poked his younger brother who slept beside him. But Mike only grunted and curled himself up like a caterpillar.

When Hollis shook Mike's shoulder hard he uncurled and slowly came awake. "What's that?" he asked aloud, for directly over their heads they heard a fumbling sound and then again a *plop—plop—plop.*

"Sh-sh-sh!" Hol hissed. "Pipe down!" He felt a tingle along his spine. This was scary. But it was exciting.

For a time the boys sat tense, listening. Then Mike said, "Are you afraid to see what's up there?"

"No, I'm not afraid." Hollis slid out of bed and clicked on the switch. Light sprang from a raw bulb, dangling on a frayed cord.

The boys kept close together as they tiptoed barefoot down the dark hall. That black opening must be the attic stair. They crept up, feeling their way along the wall.

Hollis stopped Mike with his hand. The two stood rooted. They heard something moving about, just on the other side of the attic door—they heard it plainly.

Hollis ran his hand over the wall, hunting for a light switch that wasn't there. It didn't seem sensible to barge into a strange attic in the dark.

As the boys waited, not knowing quite what to do, the gray light of morning crept through the staircase window. Outside, a bird called—two sharp notes repeated again and again. But now all was quiet in the attic.

"Let's go in," said Hollis.

He slid the bolt and slowly swung the door open on rusty hinges that squeaked. The boys saw a small room under a low, slanting roof. It was lighted dimly by just one little window. Beyond a brick chimney, the dark

14

corners were lumpy with boxes and bundles. Nothing moved in the shadows.

Hollis peeked behind a trunk. "Where did the thing go?" he whispered. He looked at the boxes and bundles. "I wonder who owns these?"

"Probably the people who were living here," said Mike. "Maybe Dad told them we wouldn't be using the attic. They probably didn't have time to . . ."

Hollis cut in. "Golly ding! Look at this." He pointed to a row of smudges that ran across the thick dust on the floor. They were about two feet apart.

"Are those footprints?" Mike asked.

"Well, not shoe prints," Hol decided. "They might be footprints of some sort. But where is the thing that made them? How could it get in or out? Just this one room. No other doors or cubbyholes."

"How about the window?" Mike asked.

Hol looked closely at the window sill and said, "There aren't any marks in the dust. And nothing that big could get through this little window without even touching the sill."

"That's right," said Mike. "But I think anyone who wanted to could climb that tree out there and crawl through the window. Let's try it sometime today—just for fun."

Hol examined the catch on the window and found it broken. They stuck their heads into the chill outdoors. They were looking straight into the widespread branches of a butternut tree.

"I'm freezing," Mike said. "It's awful early. Let's go back to bed."

Hollis closed the window and bolted the attic door before he followed Mike down the stair. Now what caused that racket? Bats? Mice or rats? No! That sound moved across the floor like something big.

Mike jumped into bed and buried himself under the covers until only a tuft of sandy hair showed.

Hollis climbed in slowly. "A real, live mystery in the attic," he said. "On our very first night! And I thought this was going to be a dull summer."

"Aw, Hol!" Mike's sleepy voice was muffled by the covers. "We heard a noise, that's all. It was probably nothing much. You just want it to be a big mystery."

Hol paid no attention to Mike. "I'm dead sure some large live thing was up there. Now how did it get in and out again with the door bolted?" But he was only talking to himself. Mike was snoring gently.

Hollis felt wide awake. He watched the

sun's glow spread across the faded wallpaper. Not another sound from the attic. But the clink of stove lids told him that Ann, his older sister, was up. She was building a fire in that old cooking stove. They had to use it until Thursday, when Mom and Dad would bring the electric range.

Best not to tell Ann about the noise in the attic. If he did tell her she would say he was just imagining things again.

Suddenly Hol sat up and sniffed. Smoke! He could see it coming up the stair. Was the house on fire? He bounded through the hall and down the stair to a smoke-filled kitchen.

CHAPTER 2

Breakfast in the Old House

THROUGH A SCREEN of smoke, Hol saw Ann with a frilly apron tied over her jeans. She was having a fierce fight with the old iron stove. She tucked wads of paper on top of the kindling and lit them. Then she banged the lid

shut as if she were trying to trap the fire. Black smoke poured out around the lids.

Between choking coughs she said, "I have to get this stubborn thing to work somehow."

Hol's eyes crinkled with his broad grin. It tickled him to see Ann in a tizzy. She was usually so calm and sure of herself.

He opened the kitchen door to clear the air. Then he elbowed her to one side and said, "In the country, a little scout training is more useful than all your college courses."

He tucked the paper under the wood and lit it with a flourish. The chips caught and kindled a lively fire.

"What's for breakfast?" he asked.

"You'll see," Ann said. "Better get dressed. And wake Mike and Kitty, will you?"

Hollis took the stairs two at a time. Back in his room he slipped out of his pajamas and into his clothes.

"Spooks!" he shouted as he pushed Mike into the crack between the bed and the wall. Then, running down the hall to his little sister's room, he yanked the covers from her bed and shouted, "Wake up, Kitty. The sky is falling!"

How loud and hollow his voice sounded! Probably because most of the old house was unfurnished. What a racket his feet made running down the bare stair!

The kitchen was cleared of smoke now, and the good-smelling wood fire snapped and crackled. Ann stood by the stove holding a turner.

"Are we having one of your fancy jelly omelets?" Hol teased.

Ann pointed to the griddle. "Does that look like a jelly omelet?"

"What!" exclaimed Hol. "Don't tell me that in college they taught you to make good old plain pancakes."

He went into the bathroom for a quick wash and comb, coming out again just as Kitty ran down the stair.

Her red braids were flying behind her. She was humming a little song that had no tune. When she was at the right height on the stair, she reached through the rail and brushed

Hol's dark, plastered-down hair the wrong way.

"That for you," she said, "because you pulled off my covers."

Then she ran to Ann and hugged her around the waist. "Isn't this fun, living here without Mama and Papa? It's like playing house, only real."

Ann squeezed Kitty with her free arm and said, "Ever so real, honey." Then she added, "Kitty Blair, I just can't get used to the way you have grown while I've been away at school."

"I'm six now," boasted Kitty. "That's quite old."

"Oh, it's ancient," said Ann. "Now wash your face and we'll eat breakfast. Mike, are you getting up?" she called.

Mike appeared at the head of the stair. He was the only one of the Blair children who didn't run downstairs in the morning. He slept so soundly it took him hours to shake it off.

Ann poured orange juice and put a stack of steaming pancakes on the table with a

23

pitcher of maple syrup. Breakfast was jolly until she began to talk about work.

"The dining room has to be scrubbed before we settle it," she said.

"Mom told us not to be worried about cleaning," Hol reminded her. "You are just supposed to try your cooking on us. Anyway, that's what you said when you coaxed Mom to let us stay out here alone until Dad finishes the Detroit job."

"Just the same," Ann said, "Mom will be pleased if we get this furniture settled before they bring the other load Thursday. And we can't put things in place without cleaning first."

"Wasn't the family that moved out clean?" Kitty asked.

"Oh, I think the Statts were as clean as could be expected," Ann said. "Dad told us that Mrs. Statt took sick shortly before they moved out. She's in the hospital now."

"Where did they move to?" asked Hollis.

"Mr. Statt built them a new house down in town. He is the stone mason who is laying the foundation for the big schoolhouse Dad is to build."

"Are there any children in the family?" asked Mike.

"Yes, a little girl and a boy. He's about your age, Hol—maybe a little older. You should get to know him. By the way, we're to buy eggs from the Statts. So after a while, Hol, will you take that basket . . ."

"I know," Hol interrupted. "Little Holly is to a-tisket a-tasket over to the Statt hen house for eggs."

"Ann," said Mike. "Ann, listen to me." He had been tugging at her sleeve. "Did you hear the noise in the attic this morning before daylight?"

Oh bother! thought Hollis. He should have warned Mike not to mention that to the girls.

"No," said Ann. "What kind of noise?"

"Hol thinks something was walking up there. He thinks it's a big mystery."

"He would," Ann scoffed. "Or have you been trying to scare Mike, Hollis Blair?"

"No, I haven't. Honest, Ann," said Hol. "I was in bed with Mike when we both heard the noise."

"It may have been a rat or a mouse," Ann said.

"It would have to be a pretty long-legged rat to stride along like that." As soon as the words were out of Hol's mouth he wished he hadn't said them. Now the girls knew he was serious about the sound. "It may have been a loose shingle on the roof," he added.

"Of course," said Ann.

Hol chuckled. "In a high wind I'll bet this old house could flap its shingles and fly over the bay like a big bird."

Everyone laughed and Ann began to clear the table. "Let's unpack the rest of the dishes," she said. "I'll wash them while Mike and Kitty wipe them. Hollis, will you screw in the hooks for the cups?"

"Slave driver!" said Hollis. "Where are the hooks?"

Somehow, in spite of the chitter-chatter, the dishes got stacked, clean and shining, on the pantry shelves.

CHAPTER 3

A Weird Neighbor

HOLLIS found the basket behind the back door and started down the hill with Mike to buy eggs from the Statts.

"Oh, Hol, I want to go too," coaxed Kitty. "Please, Hol."

"See?" Hol said. "All summer long it's

going to be like this—a funny little sister tagging me wherever I go."

"Now, Hol," Ann scolded. "Don't make Kitty feel unwanted."

Kitty smiled at Ann and said, "I don't feel unwanted. I know Hol's just a big tease."

"My," said Ann. "You really are growing up."

"I can't even fool my kid sister," complained Hollis. He took one of Kitty's hands and Mike took the other. She twittered and chirped like a sparrow as she half walked, half skipped between them.

How big and empty the outdoors felt, here in the country! A puff of cloud drifted over Grand Traverse Bay. From the high hill they could see orchard after orchard of cherry trees. A half mile down the road a group of buildings bordered the highway.

Hollis squinted his eyes against the sun and said, "So that's the town of Acme."

"Look who came out of that shack," Mike said, under his breath. He pointed to a tumbledown house just ahead, at the foot of the hill.

A hunched old man, with spindly legs, picked his way along the path that crossed the road from the shack to the hen house. He stopped to examine a bush. Then he stooped to pull a weed. He managed to cross the road in front of the Blairs.

"Good morning," Hollis said.

The old man grunted. His head, with its long, sharp nose, jerked forward like a turtle's. He looked each of them up and down. What bothered Hol most were the small eyes that shifted from side to side.

"Wowie!" Hol exclaimed, when they were out of hearing. "I feel as if I've been gone over with a magnifying glass."

"He gives me the creeps," said Mike.

Kitty's song had stopped. She looked back over her shoulder, holding tight to Hol's hand.

"That must be where the Statts live." Hollis pointed to a small stone house that looked new. An old jalopy stood out in front. Behind the house sprawled a jumble of sheds.

A lanky boy was driving a stake into the ground while a collie dog watched him.

A plump little girl of
about five clutched a
white rabbit and, when
they turned into the
yard, she smiled at Kitty.

"Good morning," said Hollis. "Have we come to the right place to buy eggs? We're the Blairs. We've moved into the house on the hill."

"Oh, hello." The boy drawled. "Yes, this is the right place. I'm Whit Statt. Your father said you'd be wanting eggs."

"A dozen," Hollis said as he handed over the basket.

"I'll have to gather them," said Whit. "Want to come along?" His smile was friendly, and he had eyes the color of the sky at its bluest.

Hollis and Mike followed along the path to the hen house. Looking back, Hol saw that Kitty had found a playmate. She was petting the rabbit and chatting away with Whit's little sister.

Hollis stood at the hen house door and watched Whit reach into each straw nest in a row of wooden boxes.

"I think we're in for a big storm before many days," said Whit. "The weather's been so dry and still—too still." When a hen pecked his bare arm as he reached under her, he scolded. "Mind your manners, old lady. I won't hurt you. I guess she wants to set," he told Hollis.

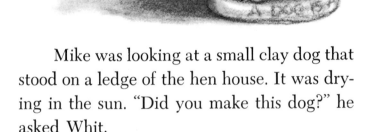

Mike was looking at a small clay dog that stood on a ledge of the hen house. It was drying in the sun. "Did you make this dog?" he asked Whit.

"Oh, that!" said Whit. "I'm not much good at it."

"I think it's good," Mike said. "Where'd you get the clay?"

"Over by the railroad track near the marsh. There's a whole bank of it there. Hard as a rock when the weather is dry like this. Have to chop it loose with an axe."

"Do you suppose I could get some?" asked Mike, looking at Hollis.

"Mike's quite an artist," Hollis explained. "He does pretty well at drawing pictures."

"Is that so?" Whit said. "Tell you what. I'll go with you for clay as soon as I finish making the rabbit hutch. That'll be sometime this afternoon."

"Oh thanks," Mike said.

Whit had finished gathering the eggs. But he still held the basket. He seemed bothered about something. He had more to say, but he didn't know how to say it.

After an awkward silence he told them, "I have a pair of tame red squirrels. Would you like to see them? They're around here behind the hen house." Whit pointed to a large wire cage.

Mike ran ahead and dropped to his knees beside it. Two squirrels scampered over the wire, flipping their tails and twitching their whiskers.

Whit looked over his shoulder at Hollis who watched from a distance.

"Hol doesn't like squirrels," Mike explained. "Once in the park when we were feeding them peanuts, a squirrel bit his finger. He had to have shots in case the squirrel had rabies. They made him awful sick."

Whit was silent for a minute. Then he said, "Too bad. He was probably holding out his hand with the peanut in his palm. That's always dangerous because the squirrel thinks the ends of the fingers are nuts."

Turning back to Hollis, Whit asked, "Don't you fellows have any pets at all?"

"No," Hollis answered. "We've never had an outdoor place for them. And Mom and Dad think a house is no place for animals."

Whit's face went blank. He handed the eggs to Hollis and put the money for them into his pocket. All easy talk had stopped.

Hol was annoyed. Had he said something wrong? Did a fellow have to own a flock of pets in order to rate? He said good-by and called to Kitty.

"Don't forget about going for clay," Mike reminded Whit.

"I'll come along about one," said Whit.

On the way home Kitty chattered about her new friend, Pudge. Only Mike listened to her. Hol was busy with his own thoughts. He couldn't make up his mind about Whit. That fellow seemed to have a chip on his shoulder.

Up the road ahead of them, they saw the old man who lived at the foot of the hill. He was puttering around his hen house, picking up stones and throwing them into a rubbish pile.

With his chin on his chest, he kept an eye on his new neighbors. Again he managed to cross the road in front of the Blairs. His shifty little eyes traveled over the three of them.

Hollis said, "A nice day."

" 'Spect so," grunted the old man.

The three Blairs hurried up the hill while the old man watched them from over his shoulder.

CHAPTER 4

A Hunt for Clues

HOLLIS began at once to tell Ann about their weird neighbor.

She bubbled with laughter. "It's like the story of the three Billy Goats Gruff," she said. "Better watch out, Hol. The troll may gobble you up."

"I remember that story," Kitty sang out. "You used to tell it to me." Then she recited, "I'm Little Billy Goat Gruff. I'm going over to the hillside to eat the green grass and make myself fat."

In the deep voice of the troll, Ann growled, "I'm coming up there to gobble you up." With the word *gobble,* she suddenly grabbed Kitty and swung her around.

Kitty screamed with joy. But Hollis said, "OK, Miss Great-Big Billy Goat Gruff. Just wait until the troll looks you over with his beady eyes. You won't enjoy it so much."

"Just leave it to Hol," Ann mocked. "If he can't find a mystery, he'll make one. He can make a mystery out of a molehill." Then she asked, "How did you like the Statt boy?"

"I don't know," Hol answered. "There's something funny about him too."

"Oh Hol!" exclaimed Ann. "You shouldn't move into a new neighborhood and from the start be suspicious of everyone you meet. But never mind that now. The water tank is empty and until there's a wind . . ."

"Fine!" Hol interrupted, grinning. "No water, no cleaning."

"It can be pumped by hand," Ann told him.

"Oh, relax," said Hol. "There are lots of things we can do without using water. A breeze will spring up in time."

Ann held out two pails. "I can't cook without water."

"Come on, Mike," Hol said. "I guess we'll have to humor her."

"I'll help," said Kitty.

"No, no, child! This is a man's job." Hollis threw back his shoulders and thumped his chest. "You stay here and help Ann."

The boys carried the pails to the windmill that stood like a giant skeleton on the peak of the hill behind the house.

Hollis was looking at the housetop while he and Mike pumped the first pail of water. "It would be easy to climb those vines to the kitchen roof and then on up to the roof of the attic," he said. "I'd like to have a look at that chimney. It must run through the attic."

Mike dropped the pump handle at once. He raced over to the tangle of vines and shinnied up them. Hollis was close behind him. It was no trick at all to climb to the attic roof and over to the chimney.

"It looks big, close up," Mike said.

"Big enough for a man to crawl through," said Hollis. "When we get the chance, we'd better examine it where it goes through the attic. This may be a way to get in and out. Let's take a look at the rest of the roof."

"What are you boys doing up there?" Ann called from the kitchen doorway. "And where is the water?" Her voice sounded cross.

Without a word, the boys scooted down the vines and in jig time finished carrying water.

The next job was to fill the wood box. Hol and Mike found the wood stored in the shed behind the house. They stopped to look through the old cans and bottles and worn-out tools that littered a workbench.

Mike started up a ladder that ran to the loft, but Hollis stopped him. "Better not do that. Ann's going to get sore if we start fooling around again. Later we'll give the whole place a going-over."

"When we go with Whit for the clay, let's ask him if he ever heard that noise in the attic," Mike said. "Maybe he could explain it, easy as pie."

"Well," said Hollis, "if we ask him at all, it will have to be in a roundabout way. How can we be sure we can trust him? If there is something mysterious going on around here he may be part of it."

CHAPTER 5

Hobo Hollow

SOON AFTER LUNCH Whit came up the road with an axe over his shoulder. His little sister and his dog, Shep, tagged along behind.

Pudge was given a warm welcome by

Kitty, who had unpacked a box of toys and set up housekeeping under an apple tree.

"Bring a pail to carry the clay," Whit called out.

Mike and Hollis grabbed a pail, and the three boys cut across a clover field. Shep raced back and forth ahead of them, chasing birds.

At the far side of the field they circled a swamp. There, where the side of the hill had been cut away to make the railroad bed, the bank glared white in the afternoon sun.

"Here we are," said Whit. He swung his axe freely, hacking away at the hard ground with slanting blows. As he loosened the chunks of clay, Hol and Mike tossed them into the pail.

"How'd you find out that this is the right kind of clay for modeling?" Hol wanted to know.

"Pop happened to slide down this bank one day after a rain," Whit told Hollis. "He noticed the clay was smooth and oily, so he brought a handful home and modeled a head with it."

"Was it a good head?" asked Mike.

The pail was full of clay now. The boys sat down in the shade of a maple tree. Whit sprawled against the tree trunk and took his time about answering.

"Well, it was the first time Pop ever tried his hand at that sort of thing. Mom told him it looked like old Mr. Roper who lives at the foot of your hill."

"Oh! So his name is Roper," said Hol. "He's an odd duck, isn't he?"

"As odd as a snakeskin hatband," agreed Whit.

Hollis had been watching Whit's face as he talked. With his slow drawl and that friendly manner, it was hard not to like him. Why not ask him about the noise in the attic? After all, Whit had lived in the old house only the week before—probably slept in the same room.

Just then they heard the shrill call of a bird—two sharp notes repeated. That was the same call that had followed the noise in the attic.

Hol's and Mike's eyes met and then their glances shot to Whit's face.

"Do you know that bird call?" asked Hol.

But Whit didn't answer. He was all ears, waiting for a second call. Then it came—an answering call from nearby in the hollow just over the bank.

Shep, who had been lying in the shade, sprang to his feet, his ruff raised, his teeth bared.

Whit grabbed Shep's collar and said under his breath, "Let's see what's over there."

The boys sneaked up the bank and peered through the tall grass into the hollow below. A spiral of smoke streamed from a stove made by balancing a sheet of metal on three stones. A can stood over the fire.

Nearby, a big man in faded blue jeans sprawled on the ground like an old sack of spoiled potatoes. His rolled-up coat made a pillow for his shaggy head. He kept blinking his bulgy eyes and watching the top of the far hill as if expecting someone.

A low growl rumbled in Shep's throat. Whit held his dog's nose to keep him quiet.

Then a small, ragged man came over the edge of the hill. A red beard circled his round face, but the top of his head was bald. He carried a brown paper sack in one hand and his hat in the other.

"Could only get oatmeal, Banjo," he told the big hobo, who wrinkled up his nose. "The guy told me to cook it in boiling water and not to stir it too much. Now, will you tell me, who would want to stir oatmeal too much?"

As he spoke, the little hobo daintily held the sack of oatmeal over the can simmering on the fire. At his last word he dumped in most of it with one swoop. Then, without even glancing at the mixture, he put the sack down and looked about for firewood.

When he wandered toward the bank where the boys were hiding, Shep suddenly jerked his nose from Whit's grasp. "Er-oop!" he barked.

The little hobo stood frozen. He stared in the direction the sound came from.

Still holding Shep's collar, Whit half jumped, half slid down the bank to the railroad bed. Hollis and Mike were close at his heels. The boys raced across the track and sank panting in the thick bushes along the fence. They watched the top edge of the bank until they were sure the hoboes hadn't followed them.

Then Whit doubled over laughing. "How to cook oatmeal in one easy lesson," he gurgled.

Mike and Hol were laughing too. "Is that a hobo camp?" Hollis asked.

"Yes. We call it Hobo Hollow. That little guy!" Whit gasped. "So fussy! And the big one —Banjo—batting his eyes like a toad in a hailstorm."

"You seemed to understand those signals," Hollis said.

"Oh, that," said Whit. "That whistle was supposed to imitate a quail's call. But it was such a bad job I knew it wasn't made by a bird and I wondered who was over there. That call should be made with a quirk at the end, like this." Whit whistled a clear, sharp "Bobwhite —ah—bobwhite."

From a nearby thicket came an answering call.

"There, hear that?" asked Whit. "That call came from a real quail."

"You are pretty clever to fool a bird," said Hol with a laugh.

"These fields are full of quail," Whit said. "I'd like to show you some of their nests, but I have to pick up Pudge and get on home." He stood up and reached for the pail of clay.

As the boys circled the swamp, Mike was

full of questions about quails, and Whit knew all the answers.

"During the winter they stay in small flocks," he told Mike. "At night they huddle together to keep warm. But they sit with their short tails pointed in so they face out. Then if they are disturbed they can fly without getting in each other's way."

Hol had been listening with only part of his mind. When they reached the clover field he took the pail from Whit and said, "Thanks for helping us get the clay. It's been fun seeing the hoboes and all." Then he suddenly said, "I've been wanting to ask you, did you ever hear strange sounds at night when you lived in the old house?"

Whit was silent for a few seconds too long. Then he said, "That old house is full of sounds. It has settled on the downhill side and sometimes it groans like an old man having a nightmare."

The answer was all right. But Hollis had noticed the pleasant easygoing look had left Whit's face.

The boys had come to the house on the hill. Whit said hurriedly, "Well, be seeing you," and long-legged it down the road.

As the Blair boys turned in at their gate, Mike exclaimed, "Say! Whit forgot to pick up Pudge."

"He has something on his mind he's not telling," Hol said. "And I'd give a lot to know what it is."

CHAPTER 6

The Trap

HOLLIS and Mike found the kitchen empty. "Ann? Kitty?" they called. No answer.

"Here's a note from Ann," said Mike. He leaned over the table and slowly read it.

Wild strawberry
shortcake for
supper. Come
help us pick:
Straight down
toward the
bay. Ann

"Here's our chance to lay a trap for clues while the girls are away," said Hol. He sprang into action. With a sack of flour in one hand he rattled through the cooking dishes until he found the sifter.

"Hurry," he called as he raced up the stair. "And bring the tablet and pencil, Mike."

The attic was just as they had left it in the early morning. Hol examined the chimney but he didn't find any openings. Plaster was chipped from the wall along the floor line. Here and there a narrow strip of lath showed. But nowhere was there a hole large enough to get even a fist through.

They examined the bundles and boxes that littered the floor. Just broken toys, tattered books, and worn-out clothes.

Hol leaned out the window to have another look at the butternut tree. "If anyone wanted to get into this attic, the simple way to do it would be to climb this tree," he said. "Yet the dust on the window sill wasn't touched."

"It sure is mysterious," said Mike.

"Something or somebody gets in and out without using the one door or the one window or the chimney. We have to find out how it is done and what is doing it."

"How?" asked Mike.

"First I'll sift this flour around over everything near the window. If anything comes through, it will have to leave tracks."

Hol had set the sifter on a trunk. Now he half filled it with flour. When he picked it up, he found a mound of flour had sifted through. "There ought to be a solid bottom hinged to this thing," he complained.

He held one hand under the sifter while he carried it, trailing flour, over to the window. He sifted flour onto everything until it danced in the air and gave the whole attic the look of a flour mill.

The job finished, Hol brushed the hair back from his forehead with his flour-covered hand. He picked up the tablet and pencil and sat down on a packing box.

"I'll make a few notes on the clues and suspects," he said. "The hoboes head the list because the call we heard, right after the sound in the attic, was the same as their signal call."

"Who else is a suspect?" Mike asked.

"Well, even Whit says Mr. Roper is as odd as a snakeskin hatband."

"He looks sneaky, all right," Mike agreed. "Let me have a sheet of that paper. I'll make my notes with a picture."

Mike drew for a few minutes with his pen. Then he looked over Hol's shoulder and said,

"Aw, you shouldn't put Whit down as a suspect."

"Have I said anything about him that's not true?" Hol asked.

"Well, maybe not," said Mike. "But just the same, he doesn't seem like a suspect. I like Whit."

"The trouble with you, Mike, is you aren't scientific. Let me see your drawing."

Mike's drawing looked very much like Mr. Roper. There were the pinpoint eyes under the shaggy eyebrows. There were the bird-beak nose, the round shoulders, and the spindle legs with big feet. He tiptoed in his socks, taking steps marked *2 ft.*

Hollis looked at the drawing and said, "The only known fact here is the distance between the footprints. You shouldn't draw the prowler until you have the facts to . . ."

A muffled sound stopped Hol. Both boys sat staring at the door. Someone was on the attic stair. Someone was listening at that door.

CHAPTER 7

A Rumor and a Hideout

WHO COULD be standing there outside the attic door—just standing there?

For breathless seconds Hollis sat frozen. Then he slipped over to the door and yanked it open.

Into the room tumbled Kitty.

"When you listen at a door, Miss Eaves-dropper, you shouldn't lean against it," Hol told her.

Kitty had an impish grin on her straw-berry-stained face. She looked about and said, "What's all this powder spread around for?"

"Now, please, Kit, don't walk across the floor there," Hol pleaded. "We are doing a little research, that's all. How did you know we were up here?"

"We saw you lean out the window when we were down by the bay."

"Be a good girl, Kitty, and help Ann while we finish," Hol coaxed. "Anyway it's too dusty for you to play up here."

"That's not the reason you want me to go away," said Kitty. She planted herself on the trunk as if she meant to take root.

"How long have you been listening at the door?" asked Mike.

Kitty just pressed her lips together and began swinging her legs. She thumped her heels so hard against the trunk that the circle of flour danced.

"Well, Mike," said Hollis, "I guess we have studied enough for today. We might as well go down now. Want to go ahead, Kit?"

"No." Then she began to chant: "I know something I won't tell. Somebody lives in a peanut shell."

"What do you know Kit? Tell us," Hol coaxed. "I'll give you a piggyback ride downstairs if you'll tell."

"OK," said Kitty, "I'll tell. There are thieves in Acme. Now give me the ride."

"Thieves!" The boys stared at Kitty. "Where did you hear that?" Hol asked.

"Pudge told me." Kitty stood up on the trunk, ready for the ride.

"Is Pudge here now?" asked Mike.

"She went home."

"Where are the thieves? Please, Kit," begged Hol. "Tell us all you know about it. then I'll give you the ride. I'll even gallop for you."

"There are thieves in the wheat field," said Kitty.

"The wheat field! What wheat field?"

"Pudge told me there are thieves in the wheat field. That's all Pudge said, so now give me my ride."

"Bring the flour and sifter," Hol told Mike. He hoisted Kitty piggyback and started down the stair. He galloped along the upstairs hall because he had promised.

Ann, hearing the clatter, called out, "Oh, boys, you should have come down to the bay instead of puttering around in that old attic. We have the most delicious wild strawberries. But I can't find the flour or sifter to make the shortcake. I've looked everywhere."

When the three came into the kitchen, Ann put her hands on her hips and looked them up and down. "I can't believe my eyes," she said. "You are powdered as white as doughnuts. Why, you've been rolling in it like babies!"

"Golly, I'm sorry, Ann." Hollis was shamefaced. "We borrowed some flour for a little research and—well, you know, it has a way of getting all over," he finished lamely.

"They were pretending they were great

detectives," spoke up Kitty. "They sprinkled flour all over the attic floor. And they called people who live around here names."

"Hollis Blair!" Ann's eyes blazed. "Are you still playing cops and robbers? Don't tell me you are trying to make a big thing out of hearing a little noise in the attic. Here we are, living out in the country for the first time. But instead of getting outdoors you poke around inside, trying to stir up a mystery in a musty attic."

Hol stood in the back door, slapping at his jeans to beat out the flour. Ann was just sore because he had carried off the flour and the sifter and made a mess. As soon as he had some real proof—proof that even she couldn't deny —he would tell her about the prowler. Then she would sing a different tune.

"Hey, Hol!" Mike was calling in a low voice. His head stuck out the window of the woodshed loft. "Come on up here."

Within seconds Hol was climbing the ladder nailed to the wall of the shed. As soon as his head popped through the opening into the loft he whistled softly. "Say, this is just right for a hideout."

"That's what I thought," said Mike.

The boys began at once to clear a space on the plank floor. They made a work table by laying boards across two sawhorses. And they used blocks from the woodpile for stools.

Mike pinned up his picture of the prowler. To the list of clues Hol added, *Thieves said to be in wheat field.*

"We had better check the nearby wheat fields," he told Mike. "If we could only find the reason why anything or anybody would want to sneak into the attic at night."

"Let's bring the clay up here and get it ready for modeling," said Mike.

"OK," said Hol. "It might come in handy."

They pounded the hard lumps into powder and wet it down. Then the smell of an oven-baked supper led them by their noses to the dining table.

Kitty had a big apron tied under her arms. She was putting the chairs around the table. Ann was dipping spoonfuls of crushed strawberries onto large squares of biscuit. Butter melted into pools and mixed with the red juice.

Damp curls tightened around Ann's flushed face. "How am I doing?" she asked the boys. "Not bad for my first shortcake is it?"

"It looks wonderful," said Hollis. Ann was OK too, he decided. She didn't stay angry for long. If the thing in the attic should turn out to be dangerous, Mom and Dad would blame him for not telling her all about it. Maybe he had better have a talk with her after Kit was put to bed.

But Kit teased and was allowed to stay up until they all went to bed soon after sundown.

CHAPTER 8

The Thing in the House

NOT A BREEZE stirred that Tuesday night. The old house was as quiet as a sleeping cat. Everyone was in bed.

Mike fell asleep as soon as his head hit the pillow. But Hol was wide awake. He wished he had had that talk with Ann—made some excuse to get her off by herself. But she surely could make a fellow feel foolish with those remarks of hers. And if he didn't prove everything in black and white she always said he imagined it.

Suddenly Hol sat up in bed, listening. Something was walking in the hall outside his room. He was sure of it. Could it be one of the girls?

He slid out of bed and peered around the half-open door. No sound now. He strained his eyes to see if anybody might be at the end of the hall near the stair to the attic. The hall was empty.

He tiptoed to Kitty's room and stuck his head in. She was safe. He could see her braids against the covers. He crept down to the living room and along the hall to Ann's bedroom. By the faint light from the window he made out her mass of dark hair against the pillow.

Hollis felt his way to the kitchen and sat down on a chair, waiting—for what he didn't know. There was no denying he had heard something walk along the hall. It was bad enough to have a thing prowling in the attic with the door bolted. But it was quite another matter to have it roam the house during the night, a thing large enough to take steps two feet long.

Maybe it was lurking behind a door this very minute, watching and waiting. Hol listened to the sounds of the house, trying to sort them out.

At first he heard only the loud ticking of the kitchen clock. Then a window shade billowed and flapped as a new wind pushed through the trees. Out behind the house, a swish-clang, swish-clang told him that the windmill was beginning to pump water. Scared as he was, Hollis thought, now Mike and I won't have to pump it.

Along with all the rustlings and tappings, he heard the squeak of the bedsprings in Ann's room. Suppose she woke up and came out to the kitchen for a drink? What would she think when she turned on the light and saw Hol—saw him just sitting there in the night? He'd better get right back upstairs, and without a sound.

His bare feet were chilled. He would crawl into bed to get warm, but he wouldn't go to sleep. No, sir. Snuggled against Mike's back he relaxed and lost himself.

The next thing he knew Ann was calling, "Get up, everybody. It's late. We've all over-slept."

Hol blinked at the sharp sunlight that flooded his room. His heart sank. He had slept through the hours he meant to be on watch. He shook Mike and headed for the attic, know-ing the sleepyhead would follow.

At the top of the attic stairs, Hol stopped short. His heart skipped a beat. He knew he had left the door bolted. Now it stood wide open. A square of sunlight spread across the white-powdered floor. What was that black thing sprawled there?

Hollis hardly noticed that Mike had joined him, staring too.

"What is it?" Mike whispered.

Hol picked up a curtain rod and poked the limp mass. Then catching it up, he swung it clear. It was a rumpled old sunbonnet.

"I'll be a flying pig!" Hollis exclaimed under his breath. "That doesn't make sense. And look, Mike. Two shoe prints in the flour on the window sill." Hol's voice was squeaky with excitement. "See? One print was made when the prowler put his foot on the sill to climb in, and the other when he was going out."

"Well, this time we know it's a man and we know how he got in," said Mike, but he didn't seemed very stirred up about it.

"Someone with big feet and heavy shoes." Hol leaned closer. "See the crisscross pattern made by the rubber heels?"

"I wonder how he got in the first night without coming through the window," Mike said.

Hol was following smudges made by flour tracked across the floor. "Mike, will you look at this!" He pointed to a small messy heap of something.

"That's oatmeal," Mike said. "And there's the paper sack it spilled out of. That little hobo

had oatmeal in a paper sack, but he didn't have big feet. So it must have been Banjo who was up here."

"And what was the little hobo doing?" said Hollis. "On the lookout maybe. We weren't awake to hear any signal calls." Then he told Mike, "The attic door was open when I came up. And last night I heard someone walk in the hall."

"If there really are hoboes sneaking around in our house at night we should tell Ann about it," said Mike. "If there really are," he added.

"Now that I have proof, I'm going to tell Ann everything," Hol said. "She'd claim that the sunbonnet and the oatmeal were probably up here all the time. But she'll have to admit there's a mystery when she sees those big shoe prints in the flour."

"O-o-h," Mike groaned. "I sat on the window sill. There aren't any shoe prints now."

CHAPTER 9

The Clay Mold

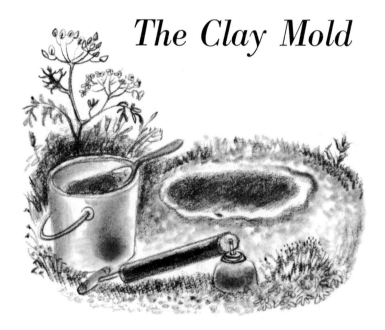

WHEN ANN called, "Breakfast is ready," the boys scurried back to their room and into their clothes.

Ann watched her brothers while they ate. Mike was usually quiet in the morning. But where was Hol's lighthearted banter? "What's the matter, Hol?" she asked. "Don't you feel well?"

"Sure, I'm fine," he told her.

"What are you boys up to?"

Mike opened his mouth to say something but at a glance from Hol he closed it again.

"I didn't sleep much last night," Hol said. "But I'm all right, honest, Ann."

"I'm going to make a batch of cookies this morning . . ."

"And I'm going to help," put in Kitty. "I'm going to stick raisins in the middle of them."

". . . but you boys should get out in the sun and get a tan," Ann went on.

Get outside? That was what Hol wanted. He could hardly wait to examine the ground under the attic window.

As soon as the boys were out of the house Mike asked, "Why didn't you tell Ann?"

"I'll tell her before the day is over," said Hol. "But there is still a chance of finding a clue she'll have to believe. Now watch your step and don't mess up any more footprints."

The boys kept on the quack grass, picking their way over to the tree. Hol's eyes gleamed as he pointed to the soil at the roots. Pressed in the ground was the print of a shoe.

"The same crisscross pattern on the heel." Hol's voice always got squeaky when he was excited. "Work shoes, I'd say."

"Now I'll have to add shoes to my drawing," Mike said. "And somehow I'll have to show the bottom of the shoe."

"Never mind that drawing," said Hol. Mike was always missing the point. "And watch out! Don't stand so close to the footprint. I wish I knew a way to preserve it."

"Why don't we just ask Ann to come out and look at it?" Mike asked. If Hol was going to be cross with him, he wasn't sure he wanted to keep on playing detective.

Hollis didn't listen to Mike. "A mold might bring out details that don't show in the print." He had read plenty of detective stories. "If we could spray the print with shellac we could make a mold with the clay. Let's see what we might be able to find over in the woodshed."

The boys hunted through the cans and bottles that cluttered the workbench.

Hollis found a gummy paste in the bottom of a can marked *Shellac*. He shook a paint-smudged bottle marked *Shellac Thinner*. "Plenty of thinner here," he said. "We're in luck."

"And we can use this." Mike held a rusty sprayer up to the light. "If we can plug up the holes," he added.

They took their finds up to their hideout. It was easy for Mike to plug the holes in the sprayer with old rags. But it took all of Hol's patience to mix thinner with the blobs of shellac. They floated around like dumplings in a broth.

Mike was making the most of his extra time by adding to his picture. "You were right," he told Hol. "I shouldn't have made the picture look like old Mr. Roper—especially since I drew it with pen and ink and can't erase. But I've figured out a way to fix it without doing it over."

"Now how can you do that?" asked Hol.

"You see, Mr. Roper's shoulders round out about the same as Banjo's chest. So I'm having my criminal go the other way. Then I'm putting the sunbonnet on Mr. Roper's head backward. That covers up his head and now he is Banjo, using the sunbonnet for a disguise."

"But, Mike . . ." Hol started to point out that they weren't sure the prowler was Banjo. And, anyway, nobody was a criminal until he

79

committed a crime. But what was the use? Mike was pretty young.

Hol glanced at the drawing and said, "But now the feet go east and the head goes west."

"That's easy to fix," said Mike. "I'll cover up the feet by drawing black shoes going west."

Mike sketched the last bit of ruffle around the sunbonnet and drew a sack of oatmeal in Banjo's hand. By then Hol had smoothed out the shellac mixture and poured it into the sprayer.

"It works," he shouted. "Bring the clay, Mike."

They scrambled down the ladder and hurried off to the butternut tree.

Hollis sprayed the shoe print so carefully that not a grain of sand was disturbed. While the shellac dried, they took the clay to the pump and added just enough water to make it pour like a thick batter into the footprint.

"There," Hol said when he had finished. "It ought not to take long for the sun to dry the clay. Now I'm going to find out how easy it is to climb this old tree." He shinnied up the trunk and climbed easily along the branch that reached the attic window.

"Look, Mike! See what I found." Hol's voice soared. He carefully untangled a thread caught on a twig. "A faded blue raveling. A raveling is a disconnected part of a piece of cloth." He had read that somewhere.

"It was probably disconnected from Banjo's pants," said Mike. "He wore old faded blue jeans."

CHAPTER 10

Thieves in the Wheat Field

"BOYS, where are you?" Ann called. "We are having a picnic lunch on the front porch."

She came through the door carrying a big plate of sandwiches and warm cookies. Kitty followed, pushing her way past the screen door while struggling with a pitcher of lemonade.

Hollis was half through eating his first cookie when he said to Ann, "You are doing all right. I'll give you double A on your cooking."

Ann and Hol smiled at each other. Ann was about to say something when they heard Pudge calling, "Kitt—e-e, Kitt—e-e!"

Kitty snatched another cookie from the plate and ran to meet her friend. They returned, arms linked, nibbling their cookies around the edges so as to save the raisins for the last.

"What is Whit doing today?" Hollis asked Pudge.

"He's mending the pasture fence," said Pudge. "Our cow broke through into the wheat field."

"Where is the wheat field?"

"It's right beside the pasture," Pudge answered.

"Naturally," said Hol. "But where is your pasture?"

"It isn't 'zackly ours," Pudge explained.

"It belongs to Mr. Roper, really. We rent it for our cow."

Ann was laughing now.

Hol kept on. "Pudge, it's fine that you have rented a nice pasture for your cow. But some day I may want to call on your cow. Where is the pasture? Point to it."

Pudge pointed to a field that rolled over the top of the hill.

So that was wheat growing in the field beside it. Nothing there tall enough to shelter a thief. But the bushes that grew along the fence would make a good screen. Hollis felt sure that anyone standing in those bushes would have a view of the attic window. He thought again of the signal he had heard just after the noise in the attic.

Then Kitty spoke up. "Is that the wheat field where the thieves are kept?" From the way she said it, you might think she was asking about field mice.

"Thieves!" Ann exclaimed. "You don't mean people who steal?"

"Yes, I do," said Kitty. "Pudge told me

about a wheat field that has thieves in it."

"Pudge, where did you hear about the thieves?" Ann asked.

Pudge had eaten all of her cookie but the center. Now she popped it with the raisin into her mouth and said, "In church."

"Did the preacher talk about the thieves?"

Pudge blissfully chewed and swallowed the raisin. Her eyes were held by that last cookie on the plate. "Nobody talked about it," she said.

Hollis was laughing now.

"But, Pudge, you just said you heard about it in church," said Ann.

"Everyone sang about it like this," said Pudge. She sang in a high, small voice:

Bring'n in the thieves,
Bring'n in the thieves,
We shall come rejoic'n
Bring'n in the thieves.

Ann laughed softly and gave Pudge a hug. "Honey, you didn't understand the words to the song. That song is about bringing in the *sheaves,* not *thieves.* Sheaves are bundles of

85

wheat. Have another cookie, Pudge dear."

"Creepers!" Hollis exclaimed. "Come on, Mike. Let's get out of here."

Now Ann was laughing her head off. "Another mystery out of a molehill," she called after Hollis.

CHAPTER 11

Telling Evidence

THE BOYS, out of Ann's sight, examined the thin layer of clay over the footprint. Hol lifted it free with his fingertips. When he turned it upside down, the dark, damp underneath surface began at once to whiten in the heat of the sun.

Hollis heaved a sigh of relief. "Here is evidence that can't be laughed off by a song," he said. "The exact markings of the rubber heel! See, it is worn down on the inside edge. And will you look at this?" Hol's voice went squeaky. "A dent made by a funny kind of metal tip on the toe. It didn't show on the shoe print but it's plain as anything on the white clay."

"Banjo probably had metal tips put on because he wore out the toes of his shoes with so much hiking," Mike decided. "If I ever get the chance, I'm going to quick look at the soles of that bozo's shoes."

"Of course," said Hol. "We must be on the lookout for the shoe that matches this cast. It is worn by the guilty party."

The boys carried the cast to their hideout and stood it on the work table along with the sunbonnet, the blue raveling, and a sample of the oatmeal.

Then they brought their records up to

date. To his list of clues Hol added, *Print of work shoe found in attic and under tree* (*see cast*). Then he placed a black mark after Banjo's name. After the note *Thieves reported to be in wheat field* he wrote, *False clue.*

Mike was having his own troubles. He was trying to sketch the sole of a shoe in his drawing.

"I'll just have to turn one foot so the bottom of it shows, even if it is not the best way to walk," he said.

"If we could only find a motive—a reason why anyone would want to get into our attic," said Hollis, frowning. "If two people had climbed through the attic window I'd think the hoboes were sleeping in there for shelter, and that maybe they forgot the oatmeal and mice got into it. But I'm sure only one person went through that window."

"Maybe Ann could help explain it," Mike said.

"Sooner or later today I'll have to tell her about it. But I think I'll talk to Mr. Statt first. Dad said in case we needed help to go to Mr. Statt."

Ann gave Hol the chance he wanted. She called from the back door, "Boys, would you like to take a walk? I'm all out of sugar—and flour too."

"OK," Hollis called.

"Flour goes so fast when we use it for floor coverings."

Hol dropped his voice and said, "She would have to add that."

The boys were on their way to the store

almost at once. They saw nothing of Mr. Roper when they passed his house.

But when they came out of the store with their groceries, there was Mr. Roper sitting on the porch. He seemed to be in a mood to talk to his new neighbors.

" 'Spect you folks is gittin' settled," he said.

"Yes, we are," Hollis answered. "Our parents will be coming tomorrow."

"Seen one of my birds up your way?" quizzed Mr. Roper.

Hol and Mike had just reached the bottom step of the porch when the question was asked. Turning to answer, Hollis said, "Why, no, we haven't. But we'll be on the lookout for it and if . . ."

Mike gave Hol a poke. Both boys had their eyes glued to the sole of Mr. Roper's shoe.

He sat tilted back in his chair, with his left knee crossed over his right. The bottom of his shoe showed plainly. There were the crisscross marks on the heel. There was the queer kind of metal tip, and he had on blue jeans.

Out of hearing, Hollis boiled over. "To think, just to think that this creepy old fellow has been sneaking into our house at night."

"I wonder what he comes for," said Mike.

"And what could he have to do with that sack of oatmeal or the sunbonnet?" Hol wondered.

CHAPTER 12

A Caller in the Storm

WHEN THE BOYS turned in at the Statt house, Shep rose from the doorstep, growling. But when they talked to him, he gave them a halfway welcome by wagging just the tip of his tail.

Hol was about to knock when he saw a note pinned to the door:

Gone to Traverse City.

Be back tonight.

Hol shifted the grocery bags to an easier position and went on with Mike. The new evidence made him boil but, just the same, it made him feel less afraid. If need be he could overpower that old man.

Mike was looking over his shoulder across the bay, as he climbed the hill. "The sky over there is a funny color," he said.

The sky did look strange. A dull, copper-colored cloud sat on the skyline. The breeze that had sprung up during the night and blown all day was turning into a gale.

The boys hurried home to find Ann struggling with the windmill.

"Come help me," she called. "Dad said if the fan is left on in a strong wind it might break."

Hollis quickly helped her pull down and fasten the lever that was connected with the racing fan.

"Now we must close all the windows. Hurry!" Ann's apron whipped around her. Her hair streamed across her face as she ran. A door banged like a shot as the wind swept through the house.

It howled all during supper. As soon as they had finished eating, the Blairs stood together at the window, watching the bay turn steel gray.

Suddenly the storm slapped the face of the old house—slapped it hard. Black clouds unloaded a sheet of rain. Hail sliced against the windows. The day turned dark.

By the steady flash of lightning, the family saw tree branches bent double in the rush of wind. The sky boomed with claps of thunder that drowned out the groans of the old house.

Yet close at hand they heard the clink of dishes. Ann put her arm around Kitty, who was frightened.

"I guess Hol put the hooks for the cups too close together," she said, laughing. "They are singing in the rain."

Then a crackling noise and a thud against

the side of the house set Kitty crying. Hol and Mike ran to the window. They could see nothing.

"Goodness," Ann said, "we don't have to stand around in the dark. Will you switch on the light, Mike? There beside you."

Mike clicked the switch, then said, "The light won't go on, Ann."

"Oh, I suppose the storm has broken down the wires," Ann said. "But it must be about over. It will soon be light again. Why, it can't be more than seven."

Kitty had stopped crying but she still clung to Ann.

"Any little girl should know what a big storm is like," Ann told her. "And this one was really a whopper, wasn't it?"

Kitty's smile was short-lived because just then Hol hissed, "There's someone on the porch. I saw him peek in the window."

CHAPTER 13

The Strange Bird

HOLLIS had seen only the blur of a white face at the window, but he knew whose it was. He flung the door open and almost bumped into the drenched old man who stood dripping in the doorway.

"Be ya all right?" quavered Mr. Roper. He held a crate in one hand and a kerosene lantern in the other. His eyes moved quickly from face to face. Then he glanced beyond them into the darkened kitchen.

"It's pretty bad weather to be out sight-seeing, isn't it, Mr. Roper?" Hol's voice sounded as angry as he felt.

"I come up this way to try to find one of my birds," said the old man. "Knew you young folks was alone and 'lectricity went off in the storm. Thought you might borrow my lantern."

Hollis was thinking, "If the old fellow really came to offer help he would have knocked on the door instead of spying on us."

"Oh, you are our nearest neighbor," Ann was saying. "You're kind to bring the lantern—

in this awful weather, too. Won't you sit down?"

"No, I won't set," said Mr. Roper. "Looks like the storm has eased. Mayhaps you'll need the lantern tonight." He left it beside the door and turned to leave. "I'll be gittin' on to look for my bird. 'Scaped this morning. A branch broke off your butternut tree. Worst storm I ever did see."

The Blairs went out onto the kitchen porch and watched Mr. Roper leave, picking his way around the puddles. He was wearing storm boots, Hol noticed. No chance to check the clay mold with prints made by his work shoes.

"Hol, you were rude to him," Ann scolded. "It's not like you. What's gotten into you? It was kind of him to leave his lantern."

Hol dropped his voice and said, "I want a chance to talk to you alone."

The sun was in the sky again. Everything was washed clean by the storm. Streams of water rushed down the gullies they had dug for themselves.

"I want to see just what happened to the butternut tree," said Mike.

"Let's all take off our shoes and go exploring," Ann suggested.

Kitty's eyes lit up. She quickly slid off her sandals without unbuckling them.

Mike ran around the corner of the house, ahead of the others. "The great big branch that went up to the attic window has split off from the trunk," he called. "It blew way over by the woodshed."

"What a shame," said Ann. "Now the old thing is lopsided."

Hollis was thinking, "Now no one can climb into the attic by that branch."

"Gracious!" exclaimed Ann. "What's that doleful thing sitting on the rail of the porch? It looks as if it swooped out of a bad dream."

A mass of feathers hung like an old mop, rather than sat, over the post. Long, stiff feathers fanned out from its legs. As the Blairs drew near, it watched them with red, bleary eyes.

"It looks sick," said Ann. "And it's badly

beaten by the storm. What do you make of it, Hol?"

"Well, I'd say it belongs to the bird kingdom," Hol decided.

"Maybe that's the bird Mr. Roper was looking for," Ann said.

"When he told us one of his birds had escaped, I thought he was talking about his chickens," said Hol.

"If this creature belongs to Mr. Roper, we should try to catch it and return it," Ann said.

Mike was within a few feet of it. Now, as he put out a hand, the bird took off with a whir of wings.

"Looks just like a helicopter upside down," said Hollis, laughing.

Mike and Kitty ran after the bird, but Hol stayed with Ann. "I've been wanting to talk to you about a lot of things," he told her. "But Kit is always around and anyway I was afraid you wouldn't believe me."

"And I've been wanting to have a talk with you," said Ann.

CHAPTER 14

Help Wanted

HOL SAT on the porch steps with Ann. How could he tell her about the mystery and get her to believe Old Man Roper was the prowler? Not knowing how else to start, he plunged into the middle of it.

"Ann, I'm sure someone climbed up the tree and into our attic window last night. And I heard someone walk through the upstairs hall."

"Now, Hollis!"

"I tell you, Ann, it's true. I have actual proof. I made a clay cast of the prowler's footprint by the tree. And someone left a sack of oatmeal and a sunbonnet in the attic."

"A sunbonnet and oatmeal! Hol, that's ridiculous."

Hol could feel his ears burn. "I knew you would say that. This morning we found a man's shoe prints in the flour we had sprinkled on the window sill."

"I thought you boys had something on your minds," Ann said. "I want to hear the whole story."

Hol told Ann all he knew about the mystery. And she was worried. He could see that.

"The neighborhood knows we are staying here alone," she said. "Some youngsters may be playing a joke just to scare us."

"But the man who roams about sneaks in

when he thinks everyone is asleep," Hol pointed out. "And part of the time, he walks around with his shoes off. That means he doesn't want us to know about it. And don't forget that the clay cast matches the sole of Old Man Roper's shoe. He's no youngster."

"I doubt if he would be able to climb the tree," Ann said. "And he was kind enough to leave his lantern."

"It was easy to climb the tree before the branch broke," Hol told her. "Maybe the lantern was just his excuse in case he was caught spying."

"We are not going to spend another night here without letting someone know about this," Ann said. "If we had a phone I would call Dad. I might call him from the general store."

"You could," Hol agreed. "But that would be like broadcasting. When Mike and I were down there, that store was full of men. They just sat around, taking in everything. We might better talk to Mr. Statt."

"That's a splendid idea, Hol," Ann said.

"We should do it right away. It'll be getting dark in another hour."

Hollis told Ann about the note pinned to the Statts' door. "They're probably back from Traverse City by now," he added. "Let's go."

Just over the bank, Hol and Ann came upon Mike and Kitty. The two had dammed up a ditch and were guiding streams into it until the water had spread out for yards, filling a hollow.

"We are walking down to Mr. Statt's," Ann told them. "We'll be back in half an hour. Wait here for us, will you?"

"OK," they both said. But they were so excited about their handmade pond, they hardly heard her.

When Ann and Hollis passed Mr. Roper's place, the door of his shack was open but they didn't see him. Then at the Statts' they were disappointed to find that the family still had not returned.

Ann said, "Probably they were visiting Mrs. Statt at the hospital and have been delayed by the storm. What now?"

As Hol walked toward home with Ann, he saw that she was terribly upset. "We have just this one night before Mom and Dad will be here," he told her. "We can manage."

"I don't like it, Hol. Kitty has had one bad scare already. It's not sensible to risk another."

"The prowler can't enter the attic by the tree now," Hollis pointed out. "We could lock up the house and you could sleep upstairs with Kit. We would all be within hearing of each other. If necesary, I could handle Roper."

"If we spend this night alone in the house —and I don't know what else we can do—we'll not provoke trouble in any way," said Ann. "The important thing is to get through the night without any more scares."

They had walked back as far as Mr. Roper's shack when Ann had her crazy idea. "I think I'll stop and talk to Mr. Roper," she said. "He might be able to clear up the whole matter in a minute."

CHAPTER 15

The Night Watch

HOLLIS could hardly believe his ears. Stop at Mr. Roper's shack now and tell him about the mystery! That old man was the chief suspect.

"Ann, please don't do that," Hol begged. "That would be playing right into his hands. It's like telling him to watch his step tonight because we are on our guard."

"Hollis Blair, you are wrong if you think I am going to play detective with you. Anyway, I'd like to ask him if that old mop of a bird is the one he was looking for. We should let him know that we saw it fly down the hill in this direction."

Hollis followed Ann to the door of the shack. It was still open.

"Mr. Roper, are you home?" she called.

No answer. The sun was low in the sky behind the house. As Ann and Hol stood in the long shadow they saw that the back door was open too. They could see straight through the one-room shack.

"Creepers!" Hol exclaimed. "Look what's perched on that rocker."

A one-armed rocker stood out sharply against the light from the back door. Hunched on the back of the rocker was the old bird they had seen in their yard.

"We were right," Ann said. "It's a pet and it has found its way back. Mr. Roper may still be out looking for it. Let's go home. We shouldn't leave Mike and Kit alone any longer."

They found the two still puttering around their pond. They were gathering colored stones, washed clean and bright by the rain. As soon as they got home they wanted to sort them.

Ann spread newspapers on the dining room table for their treasures. And then because the electricity was still off, she found a candle and lit it.

In the kitchen, by the light of Mr. Roper's lantern, Ann and Hol talked in hushed voices. What a relief to have Ann take the mystery seriously! Hol brought the cast of the shoe print to show her.

"I've never seen metal tips like that," she said.

By the light of the lantern they climbed the stair to the attic. Ann said nothing about the mess made by the flour. "Do you suppose we could fasten the window in some way?" she asked.

"It's a long way from the ground," Hol said. "How could anyone get up to it, now that the branch is off the tree?"

"I suppose you're right," said Ann. In the flickering lantern light she looked tired and scared.

Hollis was sorry for her. He was scared too, but he felt as alive as a riled hornet.

On the way downstairs Ann called to Kitty, "It's past your bedtime, honey."

"I don't want to go to bed until everybody does," said Kitty. She and Mike kept on sorting the stones in piles according to their colors.

"We are all going to bed now and get up early," Ann told her. "You know, tomorrow Mom and Daddy will be here. I'll have to move out of the downstairs bedroom and sleep with you. I might as well start tonight."

"Oh, goody!" Kitty squealed. "Will you tell me a story after we get in bed, the way you used to?"

"Just the way I used to," Ann promised.

"Let's wash off the sand, and to bed we go."

In their room, Hol and Mike talked under their breath.

"What would we do if we heard someone in the attic?" Mike wanted to know.

"I have a plan," Hol told him. "See, I sneaked this clothesline up here. If we can catch old Mr. Roper by surprise and tie him up, he'll have some explaining to do."

The boys were still dressed except for their shoes. Mike crept under the covers and Hol promised to wake him if anything happened.

Hol sat in a straight-backed chair and looked out the window until his head began to nod. To keep awake, he paced the floor in the dark. Several times during the long night he dozed in the chair and woke himself by falling.

A slice of moon rode high in a ragged sky. Could that light along the skyline mean morning? Thursday morning. Mom and Dad would arrive by noon. Would he ever be glad to see them!

Sitting hunched, his chin in his hands, Hol watched the first faint light creep into the sky. So far, so good.

Suddenly Hol jumped to his feet and craned his neck to look over the edge of the first-story roof. What was that thing bobbing along outside? It looked like the top of a ladder being carried by someone. It was being carried toward the attic window.

After giving Mike a hard shake, Hol grabbed a blanket and the clothesline. He raced through the hall and up the stair. Within the minute he stood flattened against the wall beside the attic window, blanket held high.

CHAPTER 16

At the Top of the Ladder

HOLLIS heard the scraping of a ladder being steadied against the house. Now someone was climbing the rungs. Hollis held his breath and waited, ready to throw the blanket over the prowler's head.

"I'll get that snooping old man if it is the last thing I do," he told himself. His heart stood still, then drummed in his chest.

The old fellow seemed to take forever. Yet he was climbing steadily. How many rungs did the ladder have? Now he must be nearly at the top.

A hand pushed open the attic window. Hollis felt a gush of cool air on his hot face. The figure stooped to crawl through, sticking a shaggy head into the attic. Shaggy head! Old Mr. Roper's head was as smooth as a doorknob. It was Banjo who had shaggy hair.

Panic seized Hol. Now he knew he was not up against a little old man. His stomach felt as if it belonged to somebody else. He wanted to run, but it was too late. The fellow was almost through the window.

Hollis swooped with the blanket and threw it over the intruder. Then he hurled his whole weight against him, causing him to grunt and fall with a thud.

Hollis jumped on top of him and felt hard muscles struggling under the blanket. How long could he hold him? Where was Mike? "Mike!" he yelled. "Come quick, Mike."

Muffled gasps came from under the blanket. What a relief to have Mike jump on him too. "Tie his feet," Hol panted.

Strangely enough, the body under the blanket relaxed and said, "Aw, lay off."

At the sound of that voice, Hollis uncovered his victim's head and looked straight into the eyes of Whit Statt!

"What's happened?" Ann called as she and Kitty came running up the stair.

Whit lay there with just his head sticking out from under the blanket, the two boys straddling him. Yet he turned his head toward Ann and said, politely, "Good morning."

"Whit Statt!" exclaimed Ann. "What are you doing up here? Hol! Mike! Get off him."

Whit sat up and brushed his hair from his forehead. He faced Hollis, who was saying, "Why have you sneaked into our house every night, Whit Statt? Explain that before those feet are untied."

"This is only the second time," said Whit.

"I climbed in by the tree yesterday. And then this morning, when I saw the branch was split off, I remembered Pop's extension ladder behind the woodshed."

"But why, Whit?" asked Ann.

"I came to get something of mine."

"Gracious, Whit, don't be so mysterious," said Ann. "If something of yours is in the attic, you don't have to sneak in for it. What is it?"

"I'll show you," said Whit.

He fished a handful of peanuts from his pocket and made a clucking sound. His eyes were fixed on the far corner of the room. It was still too early for full daylight. The Blairs squinted their eyes, peering into the shadows.

A small brown form flattened itself and slid out of a crack between the wall and the floor. The furry creature flew, or rather, took flying leaps toward Whit. It plop-plop-plopped across the floor in broad jumps. Its flat tail stuck out straight. Up Whit's leg it ran.

CHAPTER 17

Explanations

WHEN the little animal took flying leaps up Whit's leg, Kitty squealed.

Mike said, "Gol-lee!"

And Ann said with a short laugh, "A flying squirrel!"

"Yes, here comes the other one," said Whit. "I kept this pair up here before we moved. I took to leaving the cage door open at night so they'd have room to run around. Then one night they moved their nest through that crack into the wall."

"They are charming little things," said Ann, "and so tame."

"Since you catch them without any trouble, why did you leave them here when you moved?" Hol asked.

"They have young ones in the wall," Whit answered. "Now they're old enough to come out. I thought I might be able to take the family home yesterday. But when the babies didn't show up, I left oatmeal for them and decided to try again this morning. Flying squirrels are lively during the night and at dusk, but they sleep through the bright day-light."

"Why didn't you just tell us they were here?" asked Mike. "I'd like to take care of them for you."

"I planned to tell you about them when you came for eggs." Whit was looking at Hol. "But Mike said you didn't like squirrels. And you said your folks thought a house was no place for animals."

"We heard the squirrels on our very first night," Mike said. "They sounded like some big thing walking."

"When you asked about noises in the house, I wondered if you had heard these little rascals leaping about." As he spoke, Whit stroked soft brown fur with a forefinger. "I suppose I should have told you about them."

"It would have saved us a lot of worry, Whit," Ann said.

"I'm sorry," said Whit. "It just seemed easier to come and get them without saying anything. I've climbed up the tree and in that window hundreds of times."

"We were scared out of our wits during the storm," Ann said, laughing. "The branch off the tree fell against the house and the lights wouldn't turn on. But Mr. Roper came and loaned us his lantern. He was looking for one of his birds, he said."

"Yes, he had everyone on the lookout for that fancy old pigeon," said Whit. "And that was like him to bring the lantern. He has a heart as big as a barn."

"We caught him looking through the window before he offered his lantern," put in Hol.

Whit snickered. "That's like him, too. Mr. Roper is nosy all right. Mom says it's just that his life is empty. He gets too interested in other people's affairs."

"That's usually the case," Ann agreed.

"But he sure was a good neighbor to Mom after she took sick," Whit went on. "When Pop would be out on a job and I was at school, Mr. Roper climbed the hill every day to see if there was anything Mom wanted."

"A few things are still unexplained," said Hol. He was looking at the bottom of Whit's shoes. "How does it happen that you have metal tips on your shoes exactly like Mr. Roper's? And the same markings on the heels too?"

Whit looked puzzled. "Why do you ask that?"

"Hol took a cast of your footprint," Ann said. "He checked it with Mr. Roper's."

Whit's whole face broke into a grin. "I guess every other fellow in Acme wears work shoes like mine," he said. "We all buy them at the same store in Traverse City."

Hol said nothing. He felt relieved, but he also felt pretty silly. Ann was right. He had been too suspicious of everybody.

The squirrels had been eating peanuts from Whit's hand. Now they leaped across the floor and, flattening themselves out, slid through the crack into the wall.

Whit had untied the rope around his ankles, and now he stood up. Daylight filled the attic.

"We'll enjoy watching for the baby squirrels," Ann said. "Come over this evening at dusk and we'll see if we can coax them out."

"There's just one more clue that hasn't been explained," Hol said. "I'll probably be sorry I asked. But I have to know. Why did you leave an old sunbonnet here yesterday morning?"

"A sunbonnet!" Whit exclaimed.

"It isn't up here now," said Mike, "but I

can show you a picture of it." He fished his drawing out of his pocket. "Most all the clues are in this one picture," he said proudly. "All except the old bird. I haven't had time to put that in yet."

Hol watched Whit's face. Whit was trying not to laugh while Mike explained all the clues. Why did Mike have to show that picture?

A smothered giggle made everyone look at Kitty. She was hiding her face with her hands.

"What's up?" asked Hol. "Did you have anything to do with that sunbonnet?"

"You boys were so smart, being big detectives and not letting me play with you," said

Kitty. "I wanted to mix you up. So, when I found that old thing in my clothes closet, I sneaked through the hall after you got in bed. And I threw it into the attic."

"You little scamp!" cried Hol. "So you were the one I heard in the hall. And it was you who left the attic door open."

"You almost caught me before I jumped into bed," said Kitty.

Whit no longer tried to keep his face straight. He bent double laughing. Mike and Ann joined in.

Soon Hollis was laughing, too. He felt better now. "As a detective, I'm a bust," he said.

"I don't think so," said Whit. "You caught me, didn't you? That took nerve. And you made me confess. I'd say you were a success."

"Hol has lots of courage," said Ann.

"Mom and Dad are coming today," Hol said. "Mike and I will have more time to get acquainted around here. I'd like to see those quail nests."

"That's great!" said Whit.

Mike had been working away at his drawing. "There!" he exclaimed. "Now all the clues are in one picture." He held up his sketch. "See, I put the old bird on the criminal's wrist—like a falcon, you know."